Charles M. Schulz

Everyone Gets Gold Stars But Me!

HarperCollins®

"Hey, Franklin, the teacher stuck a gold star on your paper! She never sticks a star on any of my papers."

"I couldn't get a star on a Christmas tree!"

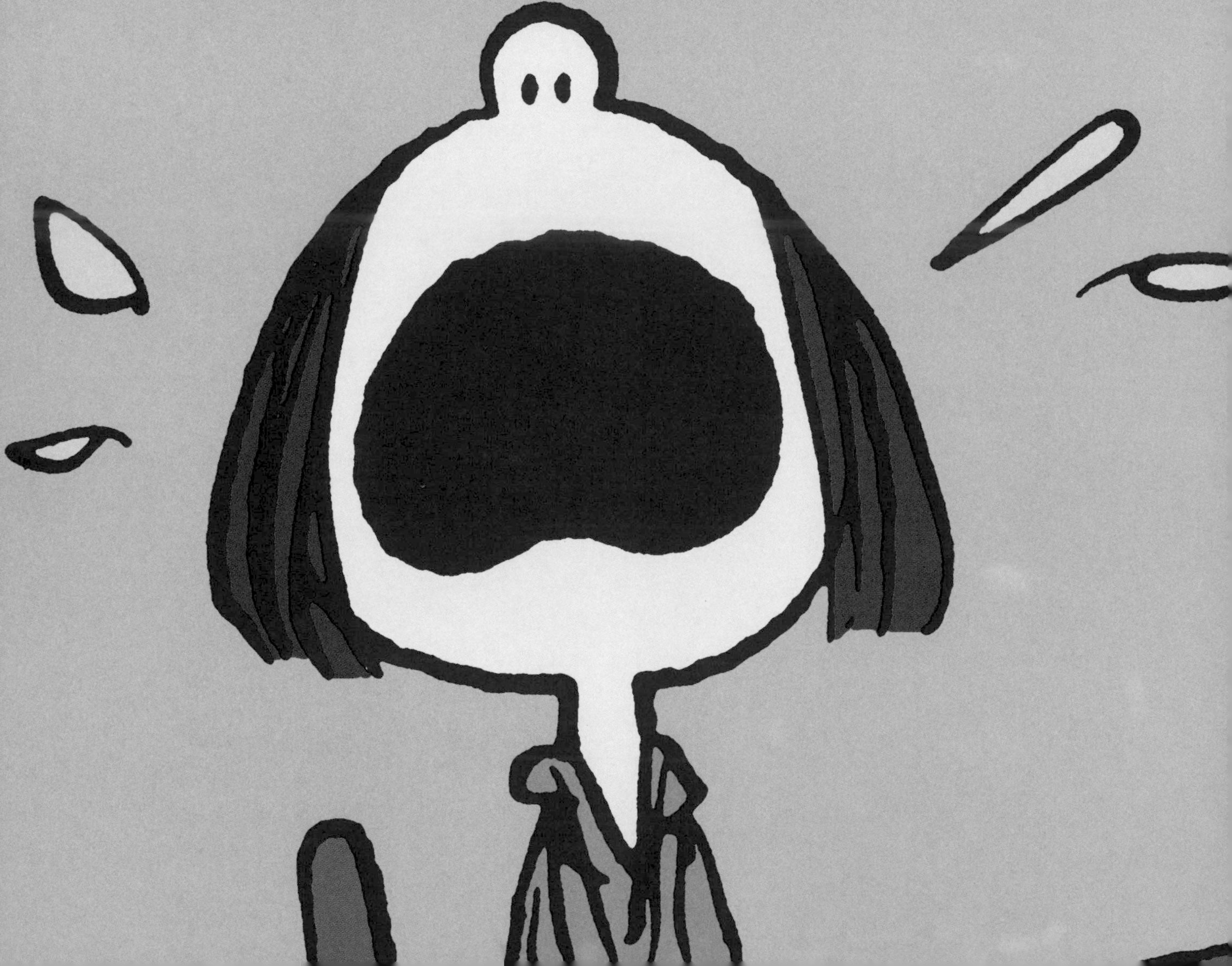

"Sorry, Ma'am!"

"I've never gotten a gold star for anything, Marcie. The teacher gives gold stars for spelling, for attendance, for drinking milk, for everything. Have you ever gotten a gold star, Marcie?"

"I got one for spelling, one for attendance, one for drinking milk, one for . . ."

"Forget it, Marcie!"

"Ma'am, may I see your box of little gold stars? Wow! Look at 'em all! Look how shiny they are!"

"The next time you stick some on any papers, Ma'am, let me know. I'll lick 'em for you!"

"Your box of gold stars? No, Ma'am, I don't have it. I put it back on your desk, remember? I wouldn't take your box of gold stars, Ma'am."

"I'm an honest person. I even have an honest face."

"Guess what, Chuck! Miss Tenure accused me of stealing her box of gold stars."

"Yes, he's right here."

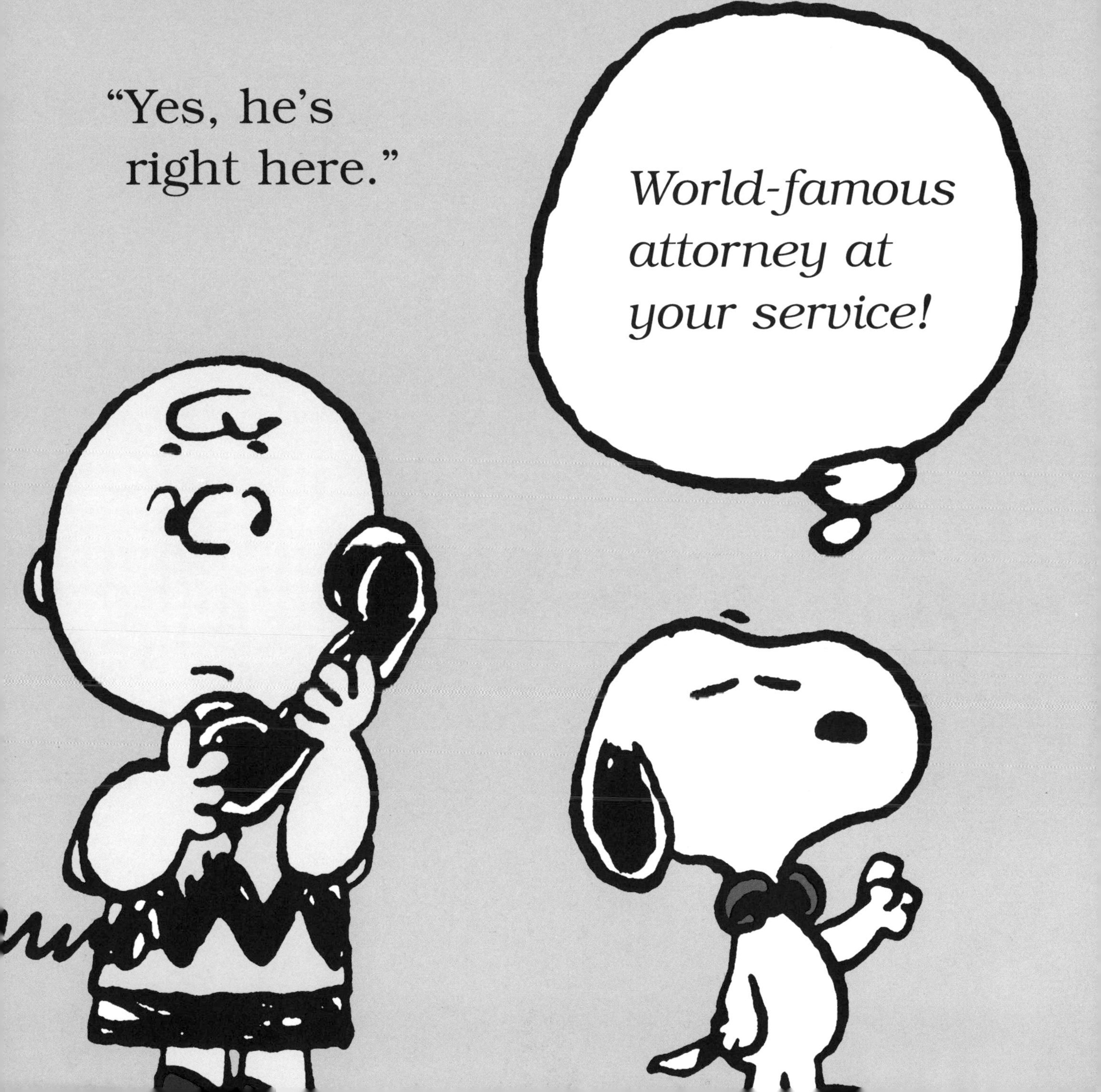

"Why would I take a box of gold stars, Chuck?"

"Maybe Miss Tenure wasn't accusing you. Maybe she was just asking."

"I didn't steal that box of gold stars, Snoopy, but I'm going to find out who did."

"You'll wear this wig and you'll sit in my seat at school. While you're doing that, I'll sneak around and find out who took the gold stars!"

"You look smaller today, Sir, and you seem quieter. Aren't you feeling well, Sir?"

"Sir, what are you doing out here in the hallway?"

"Quiet, Marcie. I'm in disguise! I'm trying to find out who took the box of gold stars."

"But I just saw you sitting at your desk."

"That's my attorney. He's also in disguise."

"Yes, Ma'am . . . I'm Hans Hansen, the new custodian. Just go on with your teaching, Ma'am. I'll sweep up a bit and empty the wastebaskets."

"Look what I found in your wastebasket, Miss Tenure . . . your box of gold stars!"

"I bet you thought one of your pupils stole it, didn't you? They wouldn't do anything like that. Especially that cute one with the beautiful hair and the freckles."

"I'm glad everything turned out all right for you, Sir."

"Snoopy did well sitting at your desk, too. He got a star on his test!"

"AAUGH!"